Acknowledgements

I wish to thank God for the opportunity he gave me in putting across another small book to the reading public.I express my eternal gratitude to my late parents, my teacher and my colleague

CONTENTS(Drama)

POEMS (poetry)

Abdul And A young couple

Husband;my darling, I love you so much I love you too, my sweet heart.

Husband; you're a beautiful girl with an attractive voice

Wife! you're a handsome man with a smiling.

Husband; whenever you smile, it toches my heart

Wife;I don't want to stay far away from you

Husband; You're the happiness of my life

Wife; I'm always happy when I see you beside me

Husband;I can't live without you

Wife; I love you more than words can say

Husband: I can't describe how I love you.

Wife: you're the only one I love.

Husband: I love you more than anything in my life

Wife: I'm together with you for ever.

Husband; only death can separate us.

Wife: of course, nothing can separate us except death

Husband: you're the hope of my life.

Wife; love is life and you're my love

Husband; my happiness is to see you happy.

Wife;my sadness is to see you sad

Husband; I feel as my heart is created because of your love

Wife; you're my husband, the father of my children.

Husband: you're my wife, the mother of my children

Wife; I do love you

Abdul; but I love reading my book.

Husband; Abdul when have you entered the parlour

Abdul;I ve been here since morning.

Wife; so,why are you hiding behind us?

Abdul; I've been reading my book, but you're disturbing me

Husband;go to the mini-library and read.this is not a place reading we're chatting here

Abdul; but I'm having a chat with my book.bye

A clever boy

The students were cheering and dancing excitedly when they were coming back from school, after completing their promotion exam.usman and sani Abdul's classmates.they were happy too and celebrating but Abdul was not celebrating."Abdul, why are you not celebrating?"usman asked. "Why should I? sitting for the exam doesn't mean passing the exam.I'll only celebrate on the day I realise that I pass my exams successfully" Abdul replied "you'd us that you haven't done well in the exam"sani said.

"I've done well and you know that I'm one of the serious student in our class, but if you do exam you have to pay for success because you might write the wrong answer thinking it's the right answer while the reverse is true Abdul answered. "We're sure that we're written the correct answer.and we must pass, join us for celebration or continue making a fool of yourself"said sani angrily."don't be proud I will only pray and wait for the day to see my results.if I pass,then I will celebrate"Abdul responded. Sani said to Abdul,"you're a fool,"there will be a day that you'ii know whether I'm fool or a cleaver boy " Abdul

A month later, the results was out and every student knew their stance sani and Usman were crying because they failed the exam and They were to repeat, but Abdul was laughing cheering and dancing because he passed the exam successfully and he was promoted to the next class. Abdul met sani and Usman crying.he asked them why they were crying thought it was the day for celebration.they remained silent and frown.he understood that they failed the exam"I have passed my exam now, between you and I,who is foolish and who is cleaver?"Abdul asked them.they kept mute. He continuesd " the day you celebrate

Was supposed to be the day for praying and today is the day for celebration.you have to learn from this simple arithmetic that hard work plus prayers is equal to su cess.you see you're now the fool and I'm the cleaver boy." He left them crying while he was dancing and cheering excitedly

POEMS

(poetry)

The day must come

The day must come
when the sun will
be static, the moon
will be asleep, the
ground will be
steaming, the
atmosphere will be
soundless, issuing
the certificate of
attending the
world to every
child of
Adam"Adam".
some will be
laughing while
others will be
crying

It's different from this stage and character.whatever you need is satisfied.all the Fridays symbols are present inevitably this would is only a field of restless battle to win the golden cup.

WE HAVE TO COME TO PASS

We have come to
pass.the would is for us
to play.our play is for
him to judge. And his
judge is the final answer.
We have come to
pass.sooner or later?
Fruitful, we hope it to be

lIFE IS TIME

CHILDHOOD

It's the morning, the time for learning how to work hard.

ADULTHOOD

It's the afternoon.the time for working hard

OLD AGE

It's the evening the time for getting tired from hard work

DEATH

It's the night the time for
going to the bed of
death.success or failure
our deed must answer
when the darkness falls

OUR LIGHT

You neither read not write, And you're no teacher, but you're the most knowledge ever,

You're the modernity of modernity, the leader of leaders, And the only way to success

You're the beauty that beautify beauty you're unique , the first and the last.the moon and the stars are your symbols that lead us to the right path, you're the mirror of life. No success with out.you can see with every part of your body. You're the answer to every question. Every creature pay home to you you're the lights of every darkness.

YES,I AM.

I'm dead to be alive before I
live to be dead thought I ve
come to pass

I'm absent in the
presence of my
absence to be
present for my
absence to be
presence the past,
the present and
the future are my
keys for opening
the door

WAKE UP

He drops pen and
paper written from
the right and from
the Left

He reject
bitterness but calls
sweetness and
aspires to smile

MY ONLY MOON

You're my only moon
that shine the earth
when the would is dark.
You're the only one.my
eyes can see my ears
can listen,my nose can
scent,my tongue can
teste,my skin can
feel,my brain can think
of,my my mind is your,

FOUR YEARS

I spent the first year
watching your step
while you remained
ignorant

I'm a bird
spreading all my
wings to different
direction without a
sigh to be myself.

I'm if you
know.i'm not if
you don't
know, I'm any
name given to
me but only
one I accept

Gratitude

to my parents

Thanks God

www.ingramcontent.com/pod-product-compliance
Lightning Source LLC
LaVergne TN
LVHW080600160826
845677LV00010B/1937
9798374712247